ANNOTATED GUIDE

TO

BASS TROMBONE LITERATURE

Thomas G. Everett

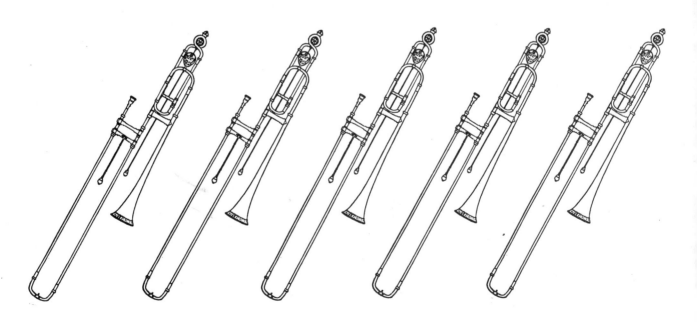

The Brass Press
Nashville, Tennessee

12-31-73

The Brass Press
159 Eighth Avenue North
Nashville, Tennessee 37203 U.S.A.

To

George Roberts, "Mr. Bass Trombone,"

who first introduced me to the

unique timbre of the bass trombone.

Table of Contents

Publisher's Note

A supplement to this text will be issued as soon as quantity necessitates. Composers and publishers interested in having their compositions or publications listed should write to Thomas G. Everett, Director, Harvard University Band, 9 Prescott Street, Cambridge, Massachusetts 02138.

The binding of this publication is intended to facilitate the addition of each supplement.

INTRODUCTION

Although the bass trombone has been a member of the symphony orchestra for over 150 years, it has only recently acquired an identity and literature as a solo instrument. Composers, teachers, and performers are becoming more sensitive to the need for original literature and study material. This may be attributed to construction and mechanical improvements including the double trigger, the realization of unique tonal qualities and technical capabilities of the bass trombone, and the appearance of many fine players specializing in bass trombone performance.

This text is intended as a reference guide to literature written specifically for the bass trombone; arrangements, transcriptions, and much of the French conservatory literature (intended for French tuba) are not included. Because the bass trombonist must familiarize himself with tenor trombone literature and technique (i.e. clef reading, slide technique, and upper register), selected publications for other instruments are listed under Supplementary Practice Materials.

Manuscripts (indicated by "MS") are available from the composers, and dates refer to the year of composition. Dates for published editions refer to the date of publication.

The following pitch indications are used throughout the text:

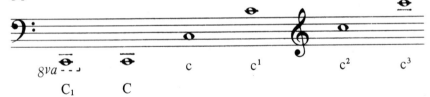

I would like to thank the many friends, composers, performers, and publishers who provided scores for examination and assisted in compiling this bibliography, especially Stephen Glover for his valuable suggestions regarding the preparation of the manuscript.

Thomas G. Everett
Harvard University, 1973

BASS TROMBONE UNACCOMPANIED

ADLER, SAMUEL. *Canto II.* Oxford University Press, 1972. Written in 1970 on a commission from Thomas Everett, *Canto II* has four short movements based on a freely-used tone row. The movements range from virtuoso and jazz styles to a moving ballad. This work exploits all facets of the bass trombone (declarative, aggressive, lyrical, and humorous) and requires a full range and technical facility. This is a difficult work for college and professional performers. *Canto II* is one of a series of unaccompanied works being written for each of the orchestral instruments. G_1 to bb^1; flutter tongue; glissandos between F valve and Bb trombone; cup mute. See Recordings: Donald Knaub.

ALLISON, HOWARD K. *Evolution.* MS, 1971. In an interesting three movement work, the soloist must perform finger cymbals and piccolo woodblock while playing trombone (second and third movements). The first two movements are dynamically varied, include wide skips, and make frequent use of the low legato trigger range. In the second movement, the melodic fragments are linked by rhythmic development to the woodblock and cymbal sounds. The last movement contains flashbacks to the earlier movements and includes the player's emotional reaction (improvisation) to cards (with designs on them) supplied by the composer. *Evolution* involves some technically awkward passages, changing meter, staging (walking from music stand to music stand), and a low tessitura. G_1 to b^1; improvisation.

BROOKS, WILLIAM. *Poempiece:* "How I fooled the armies." MS. This is a theatre piece. No other information is available.

BURTON, JAMES. *How to Compose New Music in Your Spare Time for Fun and Profit.* MS, 1971 This piece is purely for fun but possibly could be the audience's favorite work on a recital. No notated music, there are a list of activities to choose from under certain conditions. The trombonist (tenor or bass) performs with a set of bells tied to the end of the slide and the piece revolves around the ringing of the bells. A contact mike is needed for the mouthpiece. No range stipulations.

COPE, DAVID. *BTRB.* MS, 1970. *BTRB* is a theatre piece involving the "discovery" of the bass trombone. It includes producing sounds with different mouthpieces (clarinet, bassoon reed) and staging. This is an immensely effective work but requires a strong performer in this media who can act and sustain an audience's interest. The range, in the short notated section, is A to eb^1.

COPE, DAVID. *Three Movements for Solo Trombone with F attachment.* Composer's Autograph Publications, 1968. This six minute, three movement piece (slow, fast, slow), with alternating meters, requires fast mute and plunger changes. The second movement makes good use of the F trigger in the staff. *Three Movements* is well written for trombone and requires precise execution of dynamics and accents. F to bb^1; treble clef.

CROLEY, RANDELL. *Variazioni Piccola* op. 44, no. 1. Autograph Editions, 1965. This is a difficult work in cadenza style with large skips (two octaves in some cases). There is no regular meter and no time signature. The thematic material is a bit more obvious in this work than in most contemporary unaccompanied works. G'_1 to c^2; tenor clef. See Recordings: Alan Raph.

DEDRICK, CHRISTOPHER. *Lyric Etude.* Kendor Music, 1972. This short work, in singing style, is more than just an etude. A slurred melody in Eb is treated within a strict ABA form. A short double-time legato "B" section, in six flats, involves use of alternate positions, but it is not overly difficult. This is a pretty tune without use of extreme range. It may be used by a young performer or on a college recital. Bb_1 to gb^1. See Recordings: Thomas Streeter.

DEDRICK, CHRISTOPHER. *Prelude and March.* Kendor Music, 1972. Premiered by Thomas Streeter of Illinois Wesleyan University, this work is part of a series of bass trombone literature written by Mr. Dedrick. This cleverly written work begins freely with a sustained high a^1 (with optional lip trill) glissing up and then down to a low A, followed by a short phrase producing a vocal sound in perfect fifths with the trombone pitches. A unique effect is produced by humming chords while glissing down to a pedal A_1. A short Andante $\frac{3}{4}$ statement of the melody is heard before the entrance of the $\frac{4}{4}$ march. There are some long technical passages (mostly sixteenth notes) slurred in two's. The pulse of the march is broken up briefly with some $\frac{5}{8}$ and $\frac{7}{8}$ passages. G_1 to optional c^2. See Recordings: Thomas Streeter.

EVERETT, THOMAS G. *Naturally "D"* for bass trombone (with optional piano). MS, 1971. *Naturally "D"* is a short song for bass trombone in three sections: slow and singing; cadenza in fanfare style, and a return to the opening solemn theme. It is based around a D minor chord. The optional piano has random D minor chords, and the piece also allows for sympathetic vibrations from the open piano while the damper is depressed. A trained pianist is not necessary. Although it is not technically demanding, it takes a sensitive performer to interpret the work successfully. $A\flat_1$, to f^1; humming chords; glissandos.

GAY, HARRY. *Sonata.* Enrico Music, 1966. This sonata is in three movements and was written specifically for a trombone with F attachment. The first movement begins and ends with a legato line, characterized by wide skips, which is cleverly developed through rhythmic variation. The Recitative second movement (perfect ABA form) is disjunct with some fast slide work. The style is very declarative. C to a^1; changing meter.

HARTLEY, WALTER. *Sonata Breve.* Tenuto Press (Theodore Presser Co.), 1970. *Sonata Breve* is an effective short sonata in two fast movements requiring flutter-tongue, good technical facility, and ability to play wide intervals. Written in 1969 for Thomas Everett and dedicated to Emory Remington, this work is flashy sounding in typical Hartley style and makes a good recital opener or audition piece. $B\flat_1$ to $f\sharp^1$. See Recordings: Fred Boyd.

JOHNSTON, GARY. *Revelstoke Impressions.* The Brass Press, 1973. *Revelstoke Impressions* was commissioned by Stephen Glover and is dedicated to Henry Romersa. A slow introduction leads into a moderato line built on fourths while the other movements are: a tricky, peppy allegro with $\frac{5}{8}$ alternating $\frac{7}{8}$ and $\frac{2}{4}$; a very beautiful and expressive slow movement; and a rhythmic, active presto finale. Technically it moves around but is well written for the instrument. (Revelstoke is a mountain in Western Canada with unusual contrasts.) This is a fine addition to the literature. $A\flat_1$ to $b\flat^1$; Changing meter; glissando; tenor clef.

LAMBERT, SLIDE. *Three Dimensions for Bass Trombone.* Swing Lane, 1963. This is a simple three movement work in jazz phrasing. $B\flat$ to $b\flat$.

OSTRANDER, ALLEN. *Sonata in g minor* (opt. piano part on rental). Edition Musicus, 1960. This four movement work is almost in Baroque suite style, and it makes an excellent study piece for younger players. Some changing meter and technical passages are employed making excellent use of the F attachment in the staff. G_1 to e^1.

RAHN, JOHN. *Progressive Etudes.* Autograph Editions, 1969. *Progressive Etudes* has two sections: the first is pointillistic in nature with wide skips and isolated figures, and the second is a very abstract style in a special clef — the Tritone clef (each line is a semitone or a slide position). *Progressive Etudes* requires wide range, and extreme dynamic degrees; in general, it is an extremely difficult piece. D_1 to b^1; flutter tongue; contour notation; tenor clef.

RAPH, ALAN. *Caprice.* AR Publishing Co., 1963. *Caprice* is based on triplet and dotted eighth-sixteenth rhythms. This work demands a bass trombonist with a strong upper register. The last measure indicates for the performer to glissando and diminuendo from a^1 to a^2 . Ab_1 to a^2 . See Recordings: Alan Raph.

RAPH, ALAN. *Rock.* Carl Fischer, 1969. A series of rock rhythm "licks" are tied together in the lower register. *Rock* is written especially for a double trigger bass trombone. G_1 to bb ; changing meter. See Recordings: Alan Raph.

SCHWARTZ, ELLIOT. *Music for Soloist and Audience.* MS, 1970. This is not a true unaccompanied work, but features a soloist accompanied by the audience. The audience is divided into four sections and each is assigned a conductor (not necessarily a trained conductor). Each section has events (sounds) to perform; the time of events is at the discretion of each conductor. The performer has a series of events from which to choose in reaction to the audience's sounds. This is an excellent piece for lecture-recitals on new music and an enjoyable experience for both the audience and soloist. No range specifications.

SANDSTROM, SVEN-DAVID. *Disjointing.* Swedish Information Center, 1970. Written for an instrument with E valve, this work is similiar in concept to Druckman's *Animus I* and Berio's *Sequenza V.* It is dedicated to the Swedish performer Till Torsten Tufvesson and is a very difficult piece technically as well as conceptually. A seven minute work, there are no metric markings as the player performs each line in thirty seconds. Extremes of dynamics and register are used, especially in the low register. A plunger mute is required in various positions throughout the piece, and it is given it's own staff as such (above the trombone staff). There are a variety of new techniques including half-valving, singing, and humming while playing. The composer is also very particular to notate types of tongueing (even syllables), vibrato, and other sounds he desires. This piece is an excellent study in new trombone techniques and notation. (Instructions and Table of Notations are in Swedish; a translation is available from Thomas Everett.) C_1 to g^2 ; treble clef.

WILLIAMS, MARION. *Sonata.* MS, 1972. This three movement work is dedicated to Jim Ball and is intended for an instrument with a double valve (F-D). *Sonata* makes considerable use of quarter tones (not just in neighboring tones but in wide intervals), which is the most difficult aspect of this piece. There is some indefinite notation and changing meter. G_1 to e^2 (excluding effects for highest and lowest pitches possible); long slow glissandos in all registers; slow oscillation of pitch; tenor clef; subtle dynamic changes.

BASS TROMBONE AND PIANO

BARILLER, ROBERT. *Hans De Schnokeloch.* Alphonse Leduc, 1961. This French piece, dedicated to Paul Bernard, is in declarative style with a lyrical section in $\frac{5}{8}$ (alternating in spots with $\frac{2}{4}$) and requires some technique in the moving triplet section (chromatic and arpeggio). *Hans De Schnokeloch* is a humorous "folksy" work playable by mature high school students. C# to optional a^1.

BARTLES, ALFRED. *Elegy.* Sam Fox, 1970. Dedicated to Alan Raph, this 3½ to 4 minute work is part of the National Brass Solo Series. *Elegy* is in a slow, ballad style requiring good breath support and legato control. C to a^1. See Recordings: Alan Raph.

BOIZARD, GILLES. *Diptyque "Aux Statues de Bomarzo."* Edition Musicales Transatlantique, 1967. *Diptyque* is a French contest piece in two movements; the first movement is slow, and the second is fast with frequent meter changes. The performer must be quite dexterous and is required to perform flutter-tongue and lip trills. Over all, this is a difficult work. G_1 to bb^1.

BROWN, NEWEL KAY. *Postures.* MS, 1972. Written for Thomas Everett, *Postures* is a two movement work with marvelous interplay between the piano and bass trombone. The slow section features a sustained two note line in the pedal register set against a little repeating line in the piano. The "Forcefully with energy" section keeps the soloist moving around but is written well for the instruments (no fast wide slide movements). A short cantabile interlude interrupts the busy eighth note-sixteenth note line but then returns to the agitated theme. Although free use of dissonance is found, this is a conventional work and makes excellent recital material at all stages of development. Gb_1 to bb^1; flutter tongue; glissando.

CARLES, MARC. *Introduction et Toccata.* Alphonse Leduc, 1961. This is a Paris Conservatory piece. B_1 to a^1; changing meter.

CASTEREDE, JACQUES. *Fantaisie Concertante.* Alphonse Leduc, 1960. A French contest piece dedicated to Paul Bernard, *Fantaisie Concertante* is a major work with changing meter, turns, and a trigger B_1. B_1 to a^1.

COKER, WILSON. *Concerto.* Theodore Presser, 1961. See: Bass Trombone and Band.

CROLEY, RANDELL. *Divertissement.* Ensemble Publications, 1968. This is a difficult, disjointed, complicated piece. Beginning in declarative recitative style, this work consists of many varied and changing meters ($\frac{7}{8}$, $\frac{9}{8}$, $\frac{9}{16}$, $\frac{17}{16}$, $\frac{5}{4}$ + 3½, etc.), and wide skips. The composition calls for mute and a range to cover the entire horn. Bb_1 to bb^1.

DAVID, FERDINAND. *Concertino* op. 4(originally for bass trombone and orchestra). International Music Co., 1961. Although this piece, edited by William Gibson, is familiar to most trombonists as a tenor trombone contest piece, it was actually written for the 19th Century bass trombone. The instrument was smaller than the modern bass trombone and is the equivalent of today's "symphony-tenor" trombone (e.g., Conn 88H). The extremely high tessitura makes this a tiring work when performed on a full bass instrument. F# to C^2. For those interested in further information, a valuable source is "Two Early Nineteenth Century Trombone Virtuosos: Carl Traugott Queisser and Friedrich August Belke," by Mary Rasmussen. (*Brass Quarterly*, Vol. V, No. I, Fall, 1961, pp. 3-17.)

DEDRICK, CHRISTOPHER. *Petite Suite.* Kendor Music, 1972. *Petite Suite* comes with a recording of the work played by Thomas Streeter (also a recording of the Fote arrangement of Bach's *Sinfonia* for bass trombone). This little suite consists of an introduction (an unaccompanied bass trombone line echoed by the piano and then played in unison), and three short movements (slow,

fast, slow). The first movement is very well written for the instrument and the second is quite cute. This is à work for younger players; however, the phrasing, breath control, and delicate legato phrasing in the trigger and pedal register call for fine control. There are no special effects or marked passages. This creative musical material is playable by high school and non-professional bass trombonists. G_1 to d^1; duration five minutes. See Recordings: Thomas Streeter.

DILLON, ROBERT. *Concertpiece for Trombone and Piano.* MS, 1971. Part of a series of five serial pieces for solo brass, *Concertpiece* is a one movement work which begins with no time signature or regular pulse; note values are approximate and both players use a score to sychronize entrances. The free section settles into a cantabile $\frac{3}{4}$ with some cadenza-like passages and changing meter. The trombone part calls for cup mute, straight mute, glissandos, and a slide-out gliss (first to sixth positions) from f^1 to the octave above (f^2) if possible. Except for isolated passages and a very effective one line lyrical passage, the piano serves to reinforce the solo part and offers only rhythmic background to the trombonist. The trombone part, requiring an instrument with an F attachment, is well written for the instrument with few wide intervals. Various styles of trombone playing are demonstrated — lyrical, declamatory, and brilliante. Optional C# to a^1.

DUCKWORTH, WILLIAM. *Statements and Interludes.* Tenuto Press (Theodore Presser Co.), 1967. Written for Dave Sporny, *Statements* is rhythmically complicated and its five movements require much rehearsal to co-ordinate the trombone and piano parts. Changing and odd meters, wide skips, and a high tessitura make this a taxing work in an abstract style. Originally written for tenor trombone with F attachment. C to (sustained) c^2; tenor clef.

FROST, G.A. *Grand Fantasia Obligato.* Molenaar, 1964. This is a theme and variations type "war horse" which public school students could use as an etude. F to d.

GAY, HARRY. *Idilio.* MS, 1972. This 4½ minute work in Rachmaninoff style is an excellent legato teaching piece. Although not difficult, the piece sounds very "showy." The piano part is very active. C to e^1.

GAY, HARRY. *Introduction and Allegro Moderato.* Enrico Publication, 1971. Commissioned by Thomas Everett in 1969 and dedicated to Emory Remington, this is a fine work in basically lyrical style. An active piano part is set against the repeating cantabile motif in the bass trombone. The *Introduction* is a type of recitative, and, except for a short sixteenth note agitated section, the Allegro Moderato is in a singing style. Not a difficult piece, it provides an excellent setting for the high school or college recital. D to g^1.

GEORGE, THOM RITTER. *Concerto.* Rochester Music Publications, 1972. See: Bass Trombone and Strings.

GOODWIN, GORDON. *Sonata.* MS, 1971. This two movement work is unique to the majority of bass trombone literature as it is truly a piece for bass trombone *and* piano and not bass trombone with piano accompaniment. There are several solo sections for each instrument (including a long cadenza for the piano, in addition to one for the trombone). There are several other interesting ensemble effects. Some of the techniques notated are: scraping a coin on the piano strings, alternating the same pitches between Bb trombone and F attachment to produce timbre change, playing pinched sounds (marked T) in alternation with normal open sounds (marked 0), and glissandos. Parts of the first movement must be rehearsed carefully with the piano for proper ensemble. *Sonata* is a marvelous work requiring experienced and mature performers. F#$_1$ to a^1.

HARTLEY, WALTER. *Arioso.* Interlochen Press (Ferma Music Publications), 1958. Written for Byron McCulloh, *Arioso* is an experiment in sonority designed to be playable only on the slide

trombone. It is a short, slow work consisting of a legato statement in the bass trombone with some measure-long glissandos. The piano part consists of slowly moving chord clusters. Except for a crescendo to b^1 there are no great technical demands. A sensitive high school player could perform *Arioso.* D to b^1; tenor clef.

HENRY, OTTO. *Passacaglia and Fugue.* Robert King Music Co., 1963. This 7½ minute work is dedicated to John Coffey. Mostly detached playing, this work requires no special technical skills but does require strict counting and technical slide movement in the fast, changing meter fugue ($\frac{5}{8}$, $\frac{2}{4}$, $\frac{7}{8}$, at $\flat$= 276). D to g^1.

HUGGLER, JOHN. *Duo.* Composers Facsimile, 1953. This five to six minute work is not as difficult as some of Mr. Huggler's more recent music. The scoring between trombone and piano is clear and different; many times the two instruments play unison lines. Although there is changing meter and a type of free section for trombone and piano, the tempo remains Allegro Molto throughout. There are no extreme problems for the trombonist; however, the phrasing (especially some sustained pedal points) requires a mature musician. This is a very different approach to the usual solo instrument-piano type work. C to a; extreme dynamics; smear from B to a^1; both performers read from a score.

HUME, J. *The Majestic.* Boosey and Hawkes. A British contest piece. No other information is available.

IMBRIE, ANDREW. *Three Sketches.* Malcolm Music (available from Shawnee Press), 1967. Avant-garde soloist Stuart Dempster has probably been more influential in exciting and commissioning composers to write new music for trombone than any other performer in recent years. Three examples of works commissioned and premiered by him are Krenek's *5 Pieces,* Berio's *Sequenza V,* and Imbrie's *Three Sketches.* Mr. Dempster prefers to perform on the tenor-bass instrument (a large bore tenor with F attachment, commonly called the "symphony tenor"); therefore, his range is from pedal and trigger registers to the extreme upper register. He is concerned with (and a virtuoso at performing)new techniques on the trombone. For these reasons, bass trombonists are forewarned that his commissions may tend to be extremely high and, at times, not intended for the true bass trombone timbre even though they include the low and trigger registers. The piano part of *Three Sketches* has some fragmented lines, and it is a difficult part. The entire range of the tenor-bass trombone is used quite effectively with excellent dynamics. Each movement, Con Moto, Allegro, and Andante, includes some interesting effects: singing and playing two notes at the same time, trills that can be played with the valve, repeating the same note but in a different harmonic series, and purposely causing the piano strings to vibrate sympathetically to the trombone's overtones. This is a difficult work, but one of the best recent additions to the trombone literature. The technical and rhythmic subtleties are tricky. C to $d\flat^2$; tenor clef.

KAM, DENNIS. *Rendezvous II.* MS, 1967. *Rendezvous* makes use of proportional and aleatoric notations. The interaction between the trombone and piano is of prime importance and both must use a score (much rehearsal time is required). $G\sharp_1$ to $b\flat^2$; mute; flutter-tongue; humming.

KRENEK, ERNST. *Five Pieces.* Bärenreiter, 1967. This fascinating composition was commissioned by tenor-bass trombonist Stuart Dempster (see: Imbrie, *Three Sketches*). This nine minute work could easily function as an example of new techniques that can be performed by trombone and piano. Because it makes use of so many of the modern sounds and techniques, *Five Pieces* is recommended as an excellent study score for performers with limited exposure to new trombone music. This is a most challenging work but an extremely interesting one for both the performers and the audience. The work functions as a duet betweeen two equal instruments. Fascinating sonorities are created. All music is notated. Techniques include: flutter-tongue, mutes, glissandos,

micro-tones, indeterminate notation, playing with tuning slide removed, singing into instrument, hitting the mouthpiece with the palm of the hand, muttering into the instrument, etc. $A\flat_1$ to highest note possible.

LANTIER, PIERRE. *Introduction, Romance et Allegro.* Lemoine, 1965. This work is neo-romantic in style with a slow section followed by a long fast section. It is a straightforward piece but requires a technically assured player. Optional F_1 to a^1.

LASSEN, EDVARD. *Zwei Fantasiestücke* for Bass Trombone and Strings ("At Devotion" and "Dance In the Evening"). Allen Ostrander has arranged the *At Devotion* movement for bass trombone and piano (Edition Musicus, 1960). It is a fairly easy piece in slow legato style. $E\flat$ to $g\flat^1$. The complete work may be found in the Fleisher Collection of the Philadelphia Library or in the Library of Congress, Washington, D.C.

LISCHKA, RAINER. *Drei Skizzer.* Hofmeister, 1969. Not technically difficult, this three movement work (fast, slow, fast) is a very straightforward and playable piece. $B\flat_1$ to f^1.

MARGONI, ALAIN. *Apres Une Lectue de Goldoni.* Alphonse Leduc, 1964. This is a Paris Conservatory piece in 18th Century style with many scale-wise runs and arpeggios. A_1 to f^1.

MARTELLI, HENRI. *Dialogue* op. 100. Editions Max Eschig, 1966. *Dialogue* is a major work with many varied and quickly changing tempos and meters. There are several low B_1's and F's. Technically and stylistically it is a difficult and mature work. B_1 to f^1.

MARTELLI, HENRI. *Sonate* op. 87. Philippo (Theodore Presser Co.), 1956. *Sonate* is similar to but easier than *Dialogue*. It is a Paris Conservatory piece with isolated technical movement. G_1 to a^1.

MC ALLISTER, R. *First Piece.* MS, 1964. See: Bass Trombone in Chamber Music.

MC CARTY, FRANK. *Music for Trombone* op. 21. Cameo Music, 1965. This is a fine, lyrical but difficult contemporary work in two movements with frequent meter changes and an intricate piano part. At times the bass trombone plays into the piano. G_1 to C^2; mute; many glissandos; tenor clef.

MC CARTY, PATRICK. *Sonata.* Ensemble Publications, 1962. See: Bass Trombone and Strings.

MC KAY, GEORGE FREDERICK. *Suite for Bass Clef Instruments.* University Music Press, 1958. Two parts are included with *Suite*—one for tenor trombone range, and one for bass trombone or tuba. A cute programmatic work, *Suite* contains rhythmic interest without rhythmic complexities. If the lower part is used, the work is extremely low and taxing. The higher part may be used by a high school player. G_1 to f.

OSTRANDER, ALLEN. *Concert Piece in Fugal Style.* Edition Musicus, 1960. A relatively easy, conservative piece, this work contains mostly arpeggios and scale-wise runs. G to $b\flat^1$.

PETIT, PIERRE. *Wagenia.* Alphonse Leduc, 1957. *Wagenia* is a Paris Conservatory piece in slow pseudo-Wagnerian style and a consistently low tessitura. $A\flat_1$ to d; trigger B_1.

PIERCE, ALLAN. *Theme and Variation.* MS. An eight minute work. No other information is available.

PLANEL, ROBERT. *Air et Final.* Alphonse Leduc, 1968. This Paris Conservatory piece has several meter, tempo, and key changes. A very playable work. B_1 to g^1.

ROSS, WALTER. *Cryptical Triptych.* MS, 1968. Written for Per Brevig, this work makes use of graphic notation. Interplay with the piano (both use score) is important and must be carefully rehearsed (many non-metric sections). Fascinating sounds are produced by unique articulation and muting effects and interesting combinations of traditional procedures while extending trombone sound possibilities. $A\flat_1$ to $b\flat^1$.

SMITH, K.G.L. *The Happy Man.* Molenaar, 1965. This harmless piece demands only fair technical ability and some interval proficiency. It is a very obvious work for the young student. D to e^1.

SPILLMAN, ROBERT. *Concerto.* Edition Musicus, 1962. *Concerto* is a good extended work offering many different facets of bass trombone playing. The performer must have strong trigger and pedal register control for long phrasing. E_1 to f^1.

TCHEREPNIN, NICOLAI. *Une Oraison* (A Prayer). G. Schirmer, 1935. One of the earliest 20th Century pieces written for bass trombone, this work is currently out of print. It is a slow religious work with quarter, half, and whole notes; phrasing and sound are displayed. $B\flat_1$ to f^1.

TOMASI, HENRY. *Etre Ou Ne Pas Entre.* Leduc, 1963. See: Bass Trombone in Chamber Music.

VILETTE, PIERRE. *Fantaisie Concertante* pour trombone bass et orchestra de chambre (piano reduction). Alphonse Leduc, 1962. Originally written for bass trombone, orchestra, and percussion, *Fantaisie Concertante* is a major work with technical problems and some long phrases. (Optional technical figures are offered.) G_1 to c^2; changing meter; mute; tenor clef; trigger B_1's; duration: 5½ minutes.

WILDER, ALEC. *Bass Trombone Sonata.* MS (available from Harvey Phillips), 1969. Another of the outstanding works for bass trombone, this five movement piece, written for George Roberts, is as fun to listen to as it is to perform. In a third stream, pseudo-jazz style, this composition calls for much soft tongueing, flares, drops, and vigorous playing. A marvelous show piece for the bass trombone timbre. G_1 to g^1; meter changes; trigger B_1. See Recordings: Donald Knaub.

BASS TROMBONE AND ORGAN

FRESCOBALDI, GIROLAMO. *Canzoni per Basso Solo* (6 canzoni in two books for any bass instrument and continuo; first published in 1628). Verlag Doblinger (G. Schirmer). Frescobaldi did not stipulate specific instrumentation for the performance of these works but intended it for any bass-voiced instrument. These canzoni were probably accompanied by organ. They are excellent pieces in early Baroque style, and high school through professional players will find them of interest. Each canzona alternates slow and fast sections and does not contain any major range or technical problems (although the performer needs general technical facility). No articulation or dynamic markings are given in this edition. These canzoni are good for opening recitals and for providing stylistic and historical variety to programs. Range in the six canzoni varies from trigger area to middle upper register.

MULLER, J. I. *Praeludium, Chorale, Variations, Fugue* for bass trombone and organ (or piano). Edition Musicus, 1959 (originally written 1839). This is a standard in the literature. It is in typical 19th Century style and form, and is the most readily available original work for bass trombone from this era. There are no great technical demands, but it is an effective and well written composition. Bb_1 to bb^1.

BASS TROMBONE WITH STRINGS OR ORCHESTRA

ANDRIX, GEORGE. *Four Pieces for Bass Trombone and Strings.* MS, 1971 (to be published by G. Schirmer under a different title). Written for and premiered by Thomas Everett, *Four Pieces* is an outstanding work using strings in several textures (both accompaning and solo roles). The first movement is lyrical and makes use of timbre contrasts by playing G in 4th position and then in 7th position with the F valve depressed. The second movement counter-balances sustained trombone sounds with a rhythmic string part. A unique type of articulation is used in the third movement; all the ascending arpeggios are to be played with the slide moving in the same direction in neighboring positions with no tongue. This effect, which can be played properly only on the bass trombone, demonstrates Mr. Andrix's insight and inventive applications of the harmonic series to expand the technical possibilities of the bass trombone. A double trigger instrument would facilitate some of the technical problems. G_1 to $b\flat^1$; mute; glissandos between B♭ and F harmonic series by use of the valve.

BELCKE, FRIEDRICH AUGUST. *Fantasie für Bass-posaune mit Orchestra,* Op. 58 in B. (published by Gera, Blachmann?). This piece is no longer readily available although it may be found in East Germany. See information listed under Belcke, *Concertino Op. 40 for Bass Trombone and Orchestra.*

BELCKE, FRIEDRICH AUGUST. *Concertino Op. 40 for Bass Trombone and Orchestra.* Breitkopf and Härtel. Information about *Concertino* and *Fantasie* by Belcke was provided by Armin Rosin, solo trombonist with Radio Sinfonie-Orchester of the Süddeutsche Rundfunk in Stuttgart. These pieces were written for an instrument that was called a bass trombone in Belcke's day (born in 1795, he was one of the most famous trombone virtuosos of the 19th Century) but was similar to today's large bore tenor trombone. (See: Ferdinand David under Bass Trombone with Piano for further information.) This work is not readily available, but may be found in East Germany. String parts to *Concertino* are on file in the Library of Congress in Washington, D.C.

GEORGE, THOM RITTER. *Concerto for Bass Trombone and Orchestra* (piano reduction available) orchestral parts on rental. Rochester Music Publications, 1972. A major contribution to the repertoire, *Concerto* is an outstanding virtuoso work for bass trombone and orchestra (or piano). The dedication reads "for Emory Remington and Robert Brown, the master and his pupil, 1964." In three connected movements, the composer creates several moods. There are many short, quick glissandos and some very wide, difficult skips in and out of the trigger and pedal registers. The composition concludes with a fugue stated by the bass trombone. Good tongueing and accuracy are required, and the tempos and skips demand a strong player. $F\sharp_1$ to $f\sharp^1$.

KESSINGER, JAMES. *Concerto* for bass trombone and orchestra. MS. No other information is available.

LASSEN, EDVARD. *Zwei Fantasiestücke.* See: Bass Trombone and Piano.

MC CARTY, PATRICK. *Sonata* for bass trombone with string quartet or string orchestra (piano reduction available). Ensemble Publications, 1962. This fine work is presently one of the most often performed pieces in the literature. The first movement is a legato Allegretto in Dorian Mode. The second is a singing Andante and the third is Vivace. In general, legato flexibility into trigger register, octave jumps, and some fast slide movement (in last movement) are the only difficulties. A conservative work, *Sonata* is a good recital piece at all levels. Sustained (optional) E_1 to d.

MC CAULEY, WILLIAM. *Five Miniatures for Bass Trombone, Harp, and Strings* (only the score and bass trombone part are available). MS. An excellent work dedicated to Emory Remington, each

miniature demonstrates a different mood (Powerful, Peaceful, Prankish, Pensive, and Progressive). This is a difficult work that moves around and has changing meter. It is an effective work, with marvelous scoring, and is quite listenable and fun to play. E♭₁ (optional pedal B♭) to a¹; mutes.

MEYER, C. H. *Concertino pour Trombone basse avec orchestra in B.* This work, written during the 19th Century, is believed lost.

MULLER, C.G. *Concertino pour trombone de basse avec orchestra.* Breitkopf and Härtel. See information above for Belcke's *Concertino.*

POLIFRONE, JON. *Concerto* for bass trombone and chamber orchestra. MS, 1971. No other information is available.

SCHRAMM, ROBERT. *Chamber Concerto for Bass Trombone, Flute, and Strings* (piano reduction available). MS. A work in three movements, the third is a set of variations on a theme by Ralph Vaughan Williams. The second movement is a pretty legato melody in the upper register. G♯₁ to c²; flutter tongue; cup mute; tenor clef; scale-wise slide work.

SOMERS, PAUL. *Two Pieces for Bass Trombone and Orchestra.* MS. 1971. *Two Pieces,* written for Thomas Everett, begins in rock style and "regresses" to a slow 1920's type jazz. The bass trombone is prominent throughout the fast first movement in a flowing lyrical style (with some call and response sections with the orchestra) set off by a detached rhythmic orchestral accompaniment. The second movement is a slow legato in 6/8. Although very dissonant with several tone clusters (even indeterminate pitches within unison rhythms), the sparsely scored orchestra parts are not difficult. C to a¹; straight mute; indeterminate notation; high glissandos; tenor clef.

VILETTE, PIERRE. *Fantasie Concertante* for bass trombone and chamber orchestra. Alphonse Leduc. 1962. See: Bass Trombone and Piano.

BASS TROMBONE AND BAND

COKER, WILSON. *Concerto* for tenor-bass trombone (piano reduction for sale; band parts on rental). Theodore Presser Co., 1961. This is a difficult work with connected movements. Bb_1 to c^2; changing meter; high and low tessituras.

DUNN, RUSSELL. *Opus 1 for Bass Trombone.* MS, 1971. *Opus I* includes varying tempos and rubatos. It fluctuates between impressionistic (much use of 4th and 5ths) to almost jazz style chord structures and voicing. Because there are no great demands this work could easily be performed at the high school level. Contrasts are created mostly by the use of brass and woodwinds, with triplet figures. Many times the bass trombone blends with the ensemble. D to optional g^1; glissandos.

KELLY, JAMES. *Soliloquy.* MS, 1966. This a nice piece for young players. A simple legato line (phrase) is played by the bass trombone as the band slowly enters to accompany. The band parts are easy, non-technical, and rhythmically playable by junior high school groups; but careful attention must be given to long phrasing, balance, unison, and simple harmonic intonation. The bass trombone part, while simple and non-technical, can be tiring because it continues most of the time in an exposed, singing style. No effects or special techniques are called for, and nearly all the playing is done within the staff (never above a) with occasional use of the trigger register (trigger D's and E's). Optional E_1 to a.

LIEB, RICHARD. *Concertino Basso.* Carl Fischer, 1970. In the first movement, a simple repeating thematic figure keeps the solo part in the low register. No major problems are presented, but the performer should have good command of the trigger register and be able to jump down to pedal register. Dedicated to Alan Raph, this work shows the timbre of the bass trombone very well in a light vein. The three connected movements are a fast section, a ballad, and a fast section with an extended cadenza in the trigger register. *Concertino Basso* is a nice "showcase" program piece. Sustain G_1 to c^1.

TANNER, PAUL. *Concert Duet for Tenor and Bass Trombone and Band.* Western International Music, 1969. This piece includes unison passages, and call and response dialogue between the tenor and bass trombones, with an extended unaccompanied cadenza. The tenor trombone travels up to an optional f^2. There are no major problems in the bass trombone part except a few extremely low sustained parts. Db_1 to f^1.

BASS TROMBONE AND JAZZ ENSEMBLE

BAKER, DAVID. *Passion* (five saxes, five trumpets, four trombones, tuba, piano, bass and drum). Danaba Publishers (available only from Down beat Music Workshop), 1970. This jazz ballad features the bass trombone with the melody throughout most of the piece. The solo part consists of mostly jazz ♩♩ and ♩♩♩ phrasing (with optional improvisation). Lead trumpet to e^3 concert; solo bass trombone G_1 to f^1.

COCCIA, JOE. *Desiderata* (one alto, two tenor, two baritone saxes, four trumpets, four trombones, two horns, rhythm). Creative World of Stan Kenton. A medium tempo Kenton chart from the 50's, the solo bass trombone has the melody line and improvisation. Lead trumpet to eb^3; solo bass trombone B to e^1.

HOLDRIDGE, LEE. *Concerto* (alto sax [flute/oboe], three trumpets, horn, two trombones, two guitars, electric bass, organ, electric piano/harpsichord, drums, and extra percussion). MS, 1971. This "Rock Culture" concerto was written for and premiered by New York bass trombonist Alan Raph. It is now in the repertoire of the *Seventh Century,* a group that combines rock, jazz, Renaissance, and Baroque styles and techniques. *Concerto* is in two movements - Adagio and Fast. The Adagio begins in ballad style with the bass trombone unaccompanied; the ensemble then slowly builds an orchestration around the soloist. Jazz phrasing may be used for both movements. There is good rhythmic excitement in the fast section. The piece ends with a two bar bass trombone cadenza (in tempo) glissing (or chromatic with multiple tongueing) from low register to extreme upper. Eb_1 to e^2; changing meter; fast scale-wise passages.

MC VEY, LARRY. *Ballade for Trombone. Rifferendum 94. Serenade for Bass Trombone. Some Other Time* (each with standard stage band). J.M.G. Publishing Co., 1967 (available only from the composer). Written for George Roberts, these solos show off the bass trombone in a popular style. Playable at the high school level, there are no major technical demands in these compositions; the focus is on the phrasing and the relaxed dark sound of the bass trombone. *Rifferendum* is a medium up-tempo while the other tunes are basically slow with some up-tempo sections. Each arrangement may be obtained singly. G_1 to g^1. See Recordings: George Roberts.

BASS TROMBONE IN CHAMBER MUSIC

ALBAM, MANNY. *Escapade* for bass trombone and woodwind quintet. Kendor Music, 1972. A popular sounding one movement allegro work, *Escapade* spotlights the solo instrument against the standard woodwind quintet in a concerto grosso style. Throughout the work the winds play a rhythmic-accompaniment role, as the trombone plays a basically eighth-note line (with an occasional exposed, unaccompanied line). Other than some fast low register work, this is not a difficult piece. F$\sharp_1$ to f$\sharp^1$.

BRANT, HENRY. *Funeral Music for the Mass Dead* [*Credo*] for tenor trombone with bass trombone and piano obligato. Composers Facsimile Edition, 1947. This is a slow, moving, and solemn work which is not technically difficult, but demands a subtle approach. There is a large range of dynamics and long phrasings. The bass and tenor trombone have almost equal roles (the piano part is mostly chordal). Tenor trombone to e^2; bass trombone D to b^1.

CARPENTER, BUD. *Basso Bossa* for bass trombone, piano, bass, guitar, and drums. Swing Lane, 1963. In this jazz style piece the rhythm section is loaded with harmless syncopations and "F" chord changes. It may be used to introduce junior or senior high school students to simple jazz phrasing and figures. C to f.

CARPENTER, BUD. *Blues for Bass Trombone* for bass trombone, bass, guitar, and piano. Swing Lane, 1963. Similar to *Basso Bossa* by Carpenter (see above).

DEDRICK, CHRISTOPHER. *Inspiration* for bass trombone, cello, winds (clarinet, two B$\flat$ trumpets doubling flugelhorns/C trumpet, and two horns). Kendor Music, 1971. Written for Thomas Streeter by Christopher Dedrick of the "Free Design" (a popular vocal group), this three movement work is one of the most difficult and outstanding works in the literature. The texture varies from solo bass trombone cadenza to intricate full ensemble; and stylistically is quite diverse including both jazz nuances and Stravinsky type rhythms. Excellent use is made of dissonance as a means of creating tension. There are quick meter changes from $\frac{4}{4}$ to $\frac{3}{16}$ and $\frac{5}{16}$. All performers have exposed and challenging parts. A double trigger will facilitate performance of the many legato lines down to B. The soloist must have flexibility, agility, rhythmic independence, and fine control in all registers. First trumpet to concert c^3. Bass trombone G$\sharp_1$ to a^1. See Recordings: Thomas Streeter.

DEDRICK, CHRISTOPHER. *Sonata* for bass trombone, piano and percussion (8 percussion instruments played by two performers). Kendor Music, 1972. "*Sonata* is in ABA form, the first section being characterized by various meter changes. The piano acts as a percussive as well as a melodic instrument. The slow middle section features the marimba and bass trombone in canon following the initial statement of the theme. After a short cadenza, the first theme again returns with a coda to complete this unusual and colorful piece." (Quoted from the program notes of the first performance by Thomas Streeter.) F$_1$ to e^1. See Recordings: Thomas Streeter.

EVERETT, THOMAS G. *Vietnam 70* for bass trombone, tenor saxophone, and string bass. MS, 1970. *Vietnam 70* is an aleatoric and improvisational work based on the composer's reaction to war. In four sections, it requires sustained glissandos (within contour notation), and optional lighting effects. Pedal register to player's choice.

FULKERSON, JAMES. *SDTQ* for one to four bass trombones, or bass trombone, flute, string bass, and percussion. MS, 1969. The instrumentation of this work is flexible. Computer composed, it is playable by from one to four bass trombones. The composition is not technically difficult but it is in an open form (freedom within given events). Pitch is indeterminate.

GAY, HARRY. *The Coronation of Charlemagne* for four bass trombones and percussion. Enrico Music. MS, 1972. No other information is presently available on this work written for Thomas Everett.

GLASS, PHILIP. *Diversions* for two flutes and bass trombone. CMP Library (University Microfilms), 1960. *Diversions* is a tonal work in five varied movements. It is playable at the high school level; however, the bass trombonist must have a good upper register. Mr. Glass creates very clever interplay and sonorities between the flutes and bass trombone. C to b♭^{1}; cup mute; straight mute.

GRZESIK, CHRISTOPHER E. *What Do You Know!* for solo bass trombone and four bass voice singer-narrators. MS, 1972. This musical narrative commentary requires four low singer-narrators. Although the bass trombone has substantial solo passages, and the voices long quarter-note sections, the bass trombone and voice parts are integrated during most of *What Do You Know!.* Special notation for hisses, growls, and pitchless articulations are employed in the bass trombone part. Many of the singers' pitch designations are approximate. Written for Edward Foster, the bass trombonist must take great care to perform the subtle rhythms and wide dynamic range effectively. The theatre aspects of this work, the marvelous sounds created by the voices, and the clever interplay between voices and soloist make this one of the most fascinating and unique compositions in the literature. D♭ to a^1; humming while playing; glissandos using valve; contour notation.

HARTLEY, WALTER. *Sonata da Camera* for solo trombone with F attachment, oboe, B♭ clarinet, A clarinet, and bassoon. Ferma Music Publications, 1950. One of Mr. Hartley's early compositions, this fine chamber work is technically demanding for all instruments and requires precise rhythmic playing. All the instruments have a major role with a clear voicing sound. Optional C♯$_1$ to c♯^{2}; flutter tongue; quarter tones; tenor clef.

HELLERMANN, WILLIAM. *Formata* for bass trombone and four instruments (flute, B♭ clarinet, piano, percussion [vibraphone, 5 temple blocks, 3 cymbals, and woodblock]). MS, 1967. *Formata* is a difficult seven minute work in proportional notation. All parts are quite involved and all players read from the score. There are many effects, a wide range of colors, and varying dynamics. When requesting information about this work be sure to refer to the version for bass trombone. F to e♭^{2}; high tessitura; two harmon mutes; complex rhythms; tenor clef.

HINGESTON, JOHN. *Fantasia* for Trumpet (Cornetto), Bass Trombone (Sackbutt), and Organ Continuo. Musica Rara, 1971. This scholarly edition is a transcription for modern instruments of the music of Hingeston (1610-1683). Transcriptions and performances for unstipulated instruments were common practices during Hingeston's time; therefore the combination of trumpet and bass trombone in place of the 17th Century cornetto and sackbutt is justified. The *Fantasia* is in three movements and the editor has attempted to keep the music as close to the original as possible. There are no tempo or dynamic markings. F to a.

KROEGER, KARL. *Toccata* for bass trombone, clarinet, and percussion (marimba, vibraphone, tympani, gong, suspended cymbal, triangle, and temple blocks [performed by one or two players]). Alexander Broude Inc. Written for Robert D. Smith, *Toccata* is a technically and rhythmically ($\frac{2}{3}$ + $\frac{1}{4}$, $\frac{3}{4}$ + $\frac{1}{8}$, and changing meters) difficult piece. The percussion part is very difficult, and each player reads from a score. B♭$_1$ to b^1; mutes; glissandos; tenor clef.

MC ALLISTER, ROBERT W. *First Piece* for bass trombone and three trombones. MS, 1964. This composition is designed to be performed as an unaccompanied bass trombone solo, as a composition for bass trombone and piano, or as a work for bass trombone and three trombones. The four short movements are Fugue, Songs, Elegy, and Dance. *First Piece* has frequent meter changes and is effective in any of the above possible performance settings. D♭ to e♭^{1}, rhythmic security, glissando.

NISULA, ERIC P. *Trio for Bass Trombone, Violin, and Cello.* MS, 1972. This four movement work (with bass trombone cadenza movement) was written for Edward Foster (bass trombonist with the Hartford Symphony). "This entire work is characterized by lyrical lines and a shifting variety of musical expressions from medievalism to jazz . . . . The bass trombone cadenza is an effective part of the work and dynamics and phrasing may be altered in accordance with the performer's individual feeling as in any cadenza." After a short string interlude, the bass trombone plays a lyrical line in the upper register which then becomes blues style. There is fast technical playing with interval jumps. The string parts are of moderate difficulty. The length, cadenza, and amount of playing make this a taxing work for the bass trombonist. D_1 to bb^1; mute. (Quotes by Edward Foster who premiered the work.)

PEDERSON, TOMMY. *Blue Topaz* concerto for bass trombone with four tenor trombones and one bass trombone accompaniment. Date Music, 1971. This piece is similar in style to Pederson's trombone quartets (see review in *Brass World* Vol. VI, No. II, Fall, 1971). *Blue Topaz* is a slow ballad that alternates between $\frac{4}{4}$ and $\frac{6}{8}$. The solo bass trombone has some nice legato lines and a few arpeggios and scale figures. The soloist needs good sustaining power. First trombone range to bb^1; sixth trombone (bass) sustained low figures down to G_1; tenor trombone parts notated in tenor clef; solo bass trombone F_1 (optional pedal D_1) to f^1.

PEDERSON, TOMMY. *The Orators* concerto for bass and tenor trombone with three tenor trombones and one bass trombone accompaniment. Date Music, 1971. *The Orators* is an effective piece which begins with the trombones pyramiding bell tones. The accompaniment consists mostly of jazz licks behind the solo instrument. The section bass trombone functions as a basso ostinato. This jazz influenced piece is extremely technical, and all the players have taxing parts. There are changing meters, glissandos, and tempo changes. The solo parts are among the most difficult to be found; they are technically "all-over" the horn (up to c^2). There are many scale-wise runs and sustained F_1's. This is very challenging, rewarding, refreshing music — the only problem is finding a group of qualified performers. Date Music has produced a sampler record of Mr. Pederson's trombone studies and ensemble music (for further information, write Date Music). F_1 to middle upper register.

RIDDLE, NELSON. *Five Pieces* for bass trombone with two trumpets, horn, and tuba. Rumson Music (available from Dick Noel Enterprises), 1969. A light work in dance style, the movements range from a ballad to a jazz waltz. This work is not difficult for the bass trombonist, but the last movement requires slide and trigger dexterity. It shows off the bass trombone in a pop style. A_1 to f^1. See Recordings: George Roberts.

RIDDLE, NELSON. *Museum Piece* featuring bass trombone with two trumpets, horn, and tuba. Dick Noel Enterprises, 1969. *Museum Piece* is a short, one movement brass quintet in a cute popular style. The bass trombone is featured outlining chords in a light bass line. In the coda the bass trombone plays a tuba style bass line in the trigger range down to Bb_1. Younger players may enjoy this light work as there are no technical or range problems. A_1 to d^1.

STROUD, RICHARD. *The Brass Ring, "Quintet #4"* for solo bass trombone, two trumpets, horn, and tuba. Composers Autograph Publications, 1972. The *Brass Ring* is a set of five brass quintets that may be performed separately or together. Numbers one through four are available now. Number five, for antiphonal choirs, is in preparation. Written at the request of Thomas Everett, "Quintet #4" is fast throughout with changing meter but usually straight rhythms (unison rhythms or divisions of the beat). The bass trombonist performs in ensemble and as soloist (there are many exposed moving passages for the bass trombone as well as a cadenza). Although there are no range extremes, there are difficult passages; the piece requires fine players who can play together with rhythmic precision. The tuba part contains some rapid eighth note sections. G_1 to e^1; glissandos; agility.

TOMASI, HENRY. *Etre Ou Ne Pas Entre* pour trombone basse et trois trombones (piano reduction available). Alphonse Leduc, 1963. This six minute, melancholy work may be accompanied either by piano or three tenor trombones. In general, this is a very slow work with changing styles and meter in the lower bass trombone range. It is a taxing work when properly performed. $B\flat_1$ to d.

BASS TROMBONE AND PRE-RECORDED TAPE

AMMANN, BENNO. *Inventum* for tenor-bass trombone, tape, and piano (or two trombones and two pianos without tape). MS, 1971. All performers use a score in this composition which lasts nineteen minutes and nineteen seconds. A complex work, the tape part is graphically notated, while the piece is marked in five second intervals (notation is proportional). The piano parts include many special effects and there is a sheet of directions accompanying the part (written in French). The overall feel of this difficult work is complete improvisation. Unfortunately, a table of notations and special techniques for the trombone, which would be needed by anyone not familiar with new music performance, is not included. F_1 to f^2; glissandos using half valve; flutter tongue; straight mute; humming; and indeterminate notation.

BROWN, JAMES E. *Impromtu* for bass trombone and tape. Brass Press, 1973. Commissioned by Thomas Everett, *Impromtu* is for solo bass trombone interwoven with four sections of taped sound. The pre-recorded tape sounds were prepared from trombone, flute, piano, and electronic sounds. The tape and trombone at times engage in counterpoint and other times fashion something closer to a recitative. The six minute work has meter changes, a feeling of acceleration and ritard (five against three followed by three against two, etc.), and wide skips. A tape operator is required. This is a straightforward composition for tape and bass trombone, and it is not difficult to read or perform (the trombone part is in traditional notation). *Impromtu* provides an excellent introduction to tape music. $G\sharp_1$ to $g\sharp^1$.

CARRIER, LORAN. *An Electric Ginsberg* for bass trombone, voice, and pre-recorded tape. MS, 1969. Dedicated to trombonist Robert Tennyson, *An Electric Ginsberg* is an interesting work including physical movements, and even a "chance" game between the performers. The text (based on a poem by Allen Ginsberg) is for low voice. A tape operator is required. The bass trombone part is very rhythmical and technical but mostly in the staff. The soloist needs agility and a strong rhythmic sense (so as not to be confused by the tape). F to a^1; aleatoric techniques; humming; quartertones.

CORNER, PHILIP. *Big Trombone* for bass trombone and tape. MS, 1963. This an improvisational piece for bass trombone and prepared tape. The tape is composed of distorted sounds of a 1950's rock group. Pitch is indeterminate.

COX, RONN. *Diachronic* for solo B♭–F trombone and prepared Magnetic Tape. Carl Fischer, 1972 (Facsimile Edition Series). *Diachronic* was commissioned and premiered by Joel Dixon. The melodic events were derived through free use of serial technique and the electric sounds were realized on the Moog synthesizer. The trombonist plays with a score which includes graphic notation of the tape sounds as his part must be syncronized (within five second sections) with the tape. The entire upper and middle-lower range of the instrument is used, and this disjunct work requires some fast, wide intervals within technical passages. *Diachronic* is an interesting but fairly difficult work. C to d^2; using voice through the instrument; removing F slide; alternating pitches between B♭ trombone and F valve; imitating "white noise" sound; long glissandos; aleatoric and indeterminate notation; humming; flutter tongue.

DIEMENTE, EDWARD. *Hosanna II*, Seesaw Music Corp. (tape part on rental), 1972. The bass trombone and tape share equal roles in *Hosanna II* (the tape runs straight through from beginning to end; however, an assistant is needed to signal the soloist when leader sections appear). An interesting effect is obtained by altering the same pitches on the B♭ trombone and with F valve (producing different timbres). The interplay between the performer and tape sounds will vary with each performance during the indeterminate sections allowing the bass trombonist to react to the tape. Some sections are noted with metronome markings in a non-metric system, while other

sections are of undetermined speeds and lengths. This fascinating work requires no great technical demands although there are some pitches "to be played as fast as possible," and there are great contrasts in dynamics. *Hosanna II* was dedicated to and premiered by Thomas Everett. C_1 to $g\sharp^1$. flutter tongue; glissandos; special mute (a photographic lampshade).

MILLS-COCKELL, JOHN. *Reverberations* for bass trombone and four loud-speakers. BMI Canada Limited, 1966. In *Reverberations* the trombonist is accompanied by two stereo tape recorders playing through four loud-speakers (manipulated by a second performer). This fifteen minute work is in seven movements (including one movement for solo tape). The music pages may be arranged in any order (windows in each page show parts of music on another page) so that each performance will be different. G_1 to d^2 ; mutes; flutter tongue; treble clef; special effects.

MONOCO, ALFREDO DEL. *Syntagma* for tenor-bass trombone, and magnetic tape. MS, 1972. Mr. Monoco has been active with bass trombonists André Smith and Jim Fulkerson in New York and realized the tape portions of this composition at the Columbia-Princeton Electronic Music Center. The work makes use of new music techniques for trombone in the style of Druckman, Berio, Cage, etc. There is a table of notation and instructions in both Spanish and English. The trombonist's score includes a graphic chart of the tape sounds so the trombone can be synchronized with the tape. The trombonist is required to play the highest and lowest possible notes, sing while playing, create "white noise" sound, and purposely cause "beats" between the trombone and a pitch on the tape. *Syntagma* uses all registers and the performer will have to rehearse some of the effects carefully. It is a well structured piece that opens new concepts and colors for the bass trombone. E_1 to b^1; mutes (felt derby); metal plunger.

DUETS WITH BASS TROMBONE

BACHELDER, D.F. *Piece for Trombonist with F Attachment and Percussionist* (Percussion: gongs, four timpani, and vibraphone). Music Production, 1969. A very rhythmic work, the two voices are varied between unisons and counterpoint. The trombonist also plays a short cadenza. There is detached playing within changing meter which is contrasted by a short legato section. Although difficult for the percussionist, this work has no great technical demands for the trombonist. C# to b♭^{1} (optional d#^{2}); plunger; mute; flutter tongue.

BELCKE, FRIEDRICH AUGUST. *Duos für Bassposaunen* Op. 50. (Trautweir?). Written in the middle 19th Century. The above information was supplied by Armin Rosin of West Germany. No other information is available.

EVERETT, THOMAS G. *Duos for Bass Trombone and B♭ Clarinet.* MS, 1966. A two movement work, the first (Lento Misterioso) is an abstract ABA form and allows the performers to develop a section of the movement through free improvisation. The second movement, Allegretto, has many meter changes and interesting color combinations between the two instruments. Each instrument has a short cadenza. Technically *Duos* is not difficult, and extreme ranges are not used. A♭$_1$ to f^1; quarter-tones; hum chords.

GOLDSTAUB, PAUL. *Graphic I* for bass trombone and bassoon. MS, 1972. Commissioned by Thomas Everett for bassoonist Jerry Gardner, this one movement composition is written in proportional notation. Each line is fifteen seconds in length and the performers gauge their time by where the notation occurs within five second divisions in the score and by the length of the beam extending from each pitch. There is intricate chance interplay between the two parts and each performer reads from a score. Only a three bar section, an awkward "riff" figure for the bass trombonist, is notated in traditional meter. The bassoonist must have good control in all registers. This work is very enjoyable to perform and fascinating to hear. B♭$_1$ to a^1; contour notation; aleatoric notation; wide skips; glissandos; straight mute; double trigger would be useful.

HASKETT, WILLIAM. *Tenor-Bass Trombone Duets.* MS. These seven duets, in various styles, tempos, and meters, for tenor and bass trombone were written as supplementary studies to students' lessons. They are fine for developing balance, intonation, and ensemble because they are conservative and straightforward. The tenor part is mostly in the middle and high registers. A$_1$ to b♭.

MARINI, BIAGIO. *Sonata No. 9* for two bass trombones and continuo, from *Sonata, Sinfonia* Op. 8. (Available from Leslie Bassett) MS, 1626. Edited by Leslie Bassett, this is an authentic 17th Century sonata for the bass trombonist to program. The two solo parts begin in imitative counterpoint and continue to a homophonic (sustained) section. The dynamics and continuo realization are (presumably) the editor's. Organ would probably accompany the two trombones. The sonata is in G minor ending on a Picardy third. This is an excellent work in early Baroque style. First: D to c^1. Second: C to g.

MICHALSKY, DONAL. *Fantasia a Due* for bass trombone and horn. Western International Music, 1970. Written for Bob Henderson and Jeff Reynolds, this duet has various tempos and meters. There are no technical or range difficulties but the rhythm demands strong players (five against four, five against two, and four against three create an abstract structure). A$_1$ to g#^{1}; straight mute.

OWEN, NANCY. *Piece for B♭ Clarinet and Bass Trombone.* (Available from Thomas G. Everett) MS, 1970. This short, clever, modal piece has wide skips and frequent meter change. C$_1$ to g^1.

PAYNE, FRANK LYNN. *Concert Suite for Trumpet and Bass Trombone.* (available from The Brass Press) MS, 1970. This four movement suite (Rhetoric, Asymmetry, Tribute to D.S., and Toccata) was commissioned by Thomas Everett and is dedicated to Robert Levy. The second movement has frequent meter changes and tenor clef, and the third movement sounds very much like Shostakovich. The trumpet part is difficult and both players must be technically competent with good agility. The last movement is quite fast and keeps the trombonist very active in a type of basso ostinato. Trumpet to optional d^3. Bass trombone D to $b\flat^1$.

PEDERSON, TOMMY. *Ten Pieces for Tenor and Bass Trombone.* Date Music, 1971. *Ten pieces* may be purchased and performed separately or as a set. The exotic titles are: Patches, Onion Eyes, The Emery Wheel, Wheat Field Ripples, Opaque, Bug Bones, Convex, Peach Pits, Sometimes Pretty, and Ping Pong. These duets are very difficult for both voices, but they are fun to play because they are all in a light popular (almost jazz) style. The tenor player must be fluent in the upper register, while the bass part requires dexterity in the lower register (both skips and sustained playing). Trombonists will enjoy the challenge of these pieces, particularly as sight reading material. Tenor trombone (in tenor clef) to c^2. F_1 to f^1.

PEDERSON, TOMMY. *Ten Pieces for Two Bass Trombones.* Date Music, 1971. Similar in format and style to *Ten Pieces for Tenor and Bass Trombone,* these duets give both players a severe workout in the extreme low register. They are the most technically challenging duets for two bass trombones to be found. All key signatures are marked in as accidentals. Titles are: The Hitch Hiker, Busy Little Town, The Paper Plane, The Carpenter, Poos and Pools, Cashmere, The Vacuum Cleaner, Below 10th Street, The Pipe Fitter, and Looking For A Landing. Both parts F_1 to g^1.

TANNER, PAUL. *Concert Duet for Tenor and Bass Trombone and Band.* See: Bass Trombone and Band.

TRUMP, JAMES. *Piece for Bass Trombone and Clarinet.* MS, 1966. Written for Thomas Everett, this short slow duet is modal with changing meter. It is playable at the high school level. C to $e\flat^1$.

METHODS AND STUDIES

ADKINS, H.E. *Tutor for Bass Trombone.* Boosey and Hawkes (out of print). This old English method has introductory discussions on the bass trombone and elementary rudiments of music. The scales and arpeggio etudes are excellent for moving in and out of the trigger register.

BACH, J.S. *Suites for Violoncello,* Book I, *Suites Nos. 1-3;* Book II, *Suites Nos. 4-6.* Southern Music Co., 1963. Bach's *Suites* have been transcribed for tenor-bass trombone by Robert Marsteller. The mature phrasing and quality of craftsmanship found in Bach's *Suites* make these excellent musical challenges. These are valuable for developing breath control and legato.

BAMBULA, ALOIS. *Die Posaune,* Vol. 3. Hofmeister, 1962. The majority of this text consists of short major and minor scale exercises in varied time signatures, articulations, clefs, and rhythms. Some trigger markings and optional octaves (down) are suggested. Range, key facility, and rhythmic development are the strong points of these studies. The concluding section is titled "Special Etudes for Tenor-Bass Trombone in F and E♭ ."

BELCKE, FRIEDRICH AUGUST. *Six Etudes pour le Trombone de Bajo composee's et arrangee's pour le Violoncello avec accompagnement de piano.* MS, Part of the Brown Collection in the Boston Public Library (library call number 1–4-M120.18). Written in the 1840's, this is the only copy of these etudes known to this compiler. Eleven pages in length, they are characteristic of the period (mostly arpeggio and scale-wise work). The range is high (up to c^2) and there is no low trigger work. The piano part is quite easy and the score also includes a cello arrangement. These are similar to, but easier than, the Belcke *Sieben Etüden.* These etudes are not edited.

BELCKE, G.A. *Sieben Etüden für Bassposaune und Klavier,* Op. 62. Hofmeister, 1957. Edited by Paul Heber, these studies are among the few available with piano accompaniment. In varied articulations and tempos, they make extensive use of the upper register and have little valve work.

BERNARD, PAUL. *Méthode Compléte pour Trombone Basse, Tuba, Saxhorns, Basses, et Contrebasse.* Alphonse Leduc, 1960. This method, with instructions and discussions in English, French, German, and Italian, is most valuable for its "Ten Modern Studies" (by Bitsch, Dubois, Tomasi, etc.) which are among the most difficult and diverse studies to be found. Otherwise similar to Arban, this method includes discussions on history, nuances, glissandos, and technical possibilities of the bass trombone.

BLUME, O. *36 Studies for Trombone with F Attachment,* arranged and edited by Reginald Fink. Carl Fischer, 1962. This is an important technical text using all the key signatures. The first etude demonstrates thirteen possible variations that can be applied throughout the entire book. Only one etude requires low B_1. This book contains basically the original Blume, but down an octave. Valve use is edited.

BORDOGNI, MARCO. *43 Bel Canto Studies* for tuba or bass trombone. Robert King Music Co., 1972. Edited and compiled by tubist Chester Roberts, these familiar Bordogni studies in the lower register are excellent for developing breath control, phrasing, and a singing smooth legato. Slur marks are used to indicate the phrases which have been edited to make the longer ones playable in one breath.

BRIGHT, CLIVE. *Introduction to the B♭ and F Trombone.* Boosey and Hawkes, 1966. In this volume the scales (with positions marked), etudes, and little tunes are written in treble clef. This could be useful for the experienced trombonist learning treble and tenor clefs, although it is probably intended for British brass band players.

DELGIUDICE, MICHEL. *Douze Études, Rhythmiques et Mélodiques pour Trombone Basse, Saxhorn, Basse et Tuba.* Max Eschig, 1954. These etudes make use of the bass trombone in all registers (both extremes). Some of the lines are very long and technical. These are difficult and musically challenging studies.

DUFRESNE, GASTON. *Develop Sight Reading for Bass Trombone,* edited by D. Schaeffer. Charles Colin, 1954. This is the same as the trombone edition (Voisin) but an octave lower. There are unexpected twists and frequent changes of keys (within each study). The rhythms and clef changes are good for improving sight reading.

FINK, REGINALD. *Studies in Legato for Bass Trombone and Tuba.* Carl Fischer, 1969. Mr. Fink has edited and compiled legato studies of Concone, Marchesi, and Panofka. Each of the forty-two exercises includes suggested tempos, valve-slide positions, and comments on musical performance. These studies are excellent for developing breath control and phrasing. To low B_1.

GILLIS, LEW. *20 Etudes for Bass Trombone.* Southern Music Co., 1965. *20 Etudes* includes a position chart for valve use in the upper register. These studies are quite tuneful and enjoyable to play. They make use of all registers including pedal tones and several octave skips. These are excellent phrasing studies in various styles, both lyrical and technical. This book should be of value to the jazz and popular musician. Some suggested positions are marked.

GILLIS, LEW. *70 Progressive Studies for the Modern Bass Trombonist.* Southern Music Co., 1966. These systematic studies make use of the valve in the upper as well as the lower register. Positions and alternate positions are well marked as the book progresses through each valve position. Ten pedal tone studies are included. These are logical and systematic intermediate studies.

GRIGORIEV, *24 Studies for Bass Trombone,* edited by Allen Ostrander. International Music, 1970. These studies begin with exercises in C major and A minor (relative minor) and progress scale-wise in that manner to Gb major and Eb minor. Although fairly straightforward and predictable, these studies are varied in tempo, articulation, and style. They stay mostly in the middle register but there are frequent jumps down to trigger and pedal ranges. Each etude is based upon a basic rhythm and most technical passages are scale-wise. Mr. Ostrander (bass trombonist with the New York Philharmonic) has done his usual superb job of editing and notating slide positions. The long phrasing helps to develop breath-control.

HADRABA, JOSEF. *150 Stüdien Posuane,* Vol. 3, Johann Kliment, 1948. This volume (with instructions in German) includes scales and short etudes that require an F attachment. Arranged by keys, these exercises make use of all registers (except pedal), and alto and tenor clefs. There is also a section on "hot jazz." There are good scale and arpeggio exercises.

KNAUB, DONALD. *Trombone Teaching Techniques.* Rochester Music Publishers, 1964. Designed for the educator who is not a trombone major but who must instruct trombone students, this text gives excellent advice. It includes a short discussion of all aspects of playing (including the selection of instruments). The charts (harmonic series for Bb , F, E tenor and bass trombone positions), short exercises, and warm-ups are excellent.

KOPPRASCH. *Selected Kopprasch Studies for Trombone with F Attachment.* Kendor, 1964. Edited by Richard Fote, these are basically the same as the standard trombone book studies but marked for the F attachment with octave changes in places. The trigger range is the lowest used. These technical studies are good for gaining slide and valve control.

MAENZ, OTTO. *Zwanig Stüdien für Bassposaune.* Hofmeister, 1962. These difficult studies present several varied problems in each study. Wide intervals and changing meter make these studies valuable in the preparation for performing contemporary chamber, solo, and symphonic music. There is good use of the valve and several suggested positions are marked. These are among the most musical studies available.

MARSTELLER, ROBERT. *Advance Slide Technique for B♭ Tenor Slide Trombone with F and E Attachment.* Southern Music Co., 1966. There are valuable tables on temperament and frequencies, intonation, and position charts for B♭, F and E trombone (in all registers) in this text. The etudes and arrangement (of Popper, Kreutzer, Scarlatti, etc.) are excellent for the fluent execution of all regular and alternate positions. Although some of the exercises are difficult, this is the best text on the subject of slide technique.

MC MILLER, HUGH E. *A Guide to Bass Trombone Playing.* F.E. Olds & Son, 1953. Written as an introductory text, these are mostly short half note exercises in varied keys. Suggestions are given to bass trombonists on general playing and use of E valve. All valve use is notated. This was one of the earliest books published for the F and E valve instrument.

OSTRANDER, ALLEN. *Method for Bass Trombone and F Attachment for Bass Trombone.* Carl Fischer, 1967. Available only in manuscript for many years (since 1948), this was the first complete method produced by an American bass trombonist. It includes scale studies, orchestral passages, pedal tones, and etudes with E valve. Similar to *The F Attachment and the Bass Trombone,* this may be used by all bass trombonists, and it is an excellent method.

OSTRANDER, ALLEN. *The F Attachment and the Bass Trombone.* Charles Colin, 1956. These studies progress, position by position, from simple exercises to moderately difficult ones. All exercises contain suggested positions and valve use. Varied articulations and keys are used throughout. Similar to Mr. Ostrander's *Method,* this text also includes orchestral excerpts and is an excellent book for the experienced tenor trombonist who is switching to an F attachment instrument.

OSTRANDER, ALLEN. *Melodious Etudes for Bass Trombone* (arranged and edited). Carl Fischer, 1970. These melodies are taken from the *Vocalises* of Marco Bordogni. Similar to *Rochut Studies* for trombone but in a lower register, these are a valuable contribution to bass trombone studies. Mostly legato, these studies are in various tempos and keys. Slide positions and valve use is edited.

OSTRANDER, ALLEN. *Shifting Meter Studies for Bass Trombone.* Robert King Music Co., 1965. Annotated for bass trombone with double valve, these nineteen exercises are mostly in the low register (low B_1's) with odd and changing meter. These studies are for rhythmic development and preparation for the performance of much contemporary music.

OSTRANDER, ALLEN. *Twenty Minute Warm-Up for Trombone, Baritone, Bass Trombone, Four Valve Euphonium and Tuba.* Charles Colin, 1959. This warm-up consists of short patterns good for tongue and slide coordination; when transposed at appropriate places up or down an octave they become even more useful.

PEDERSON, TOMMY. *Etudes for Bass Trombone.* Date Music, 1971. These studies are in three volumes: I, Beginner; II, Intermediate; and III, Advanced. These jazz flavored etudes are among the most unique for bass trombone. They have a great deal of low register work, and as they progress they become very challenging in concept and technique.

RAPH, ALAN. *The Double Valve Bass Trombone* (a method for trombone with single valve in F, double valve in E♭, and double valve in D). Carl Fischer, 1969. This is probably the most com-

plete and thorough exercise book on all aspects of bass trombone valve performance. All aspects of playing requirements are covered with many of the exercises edited. The book is in three chapters: "The F Valve," "Double Valve," and "E♭ Tuning and Double Valve D tuning."

RAPH, ALAN. *Twenty-six Etudes for Bass Trombone.* A.R. Publishing Co. *Twenty-six Etudes* are transcribed from the vocalises of Concone, Nava, and Lampert. (Piano accompaniment is available.) The Concone exercises are similar to those for tenor trombone (keys and register are different) and are mostly slow, legato pieces in the low register.   1804272

RAPH, ALAN. *Diversified Trombone Etudes.* A.R. Publishing Co. According to Mr. Raph, these fourteen exercises should be practiced daily, once they are mastered. There are scales, slurs, intervals (with three octave jumps!), high register tongueing, and lip turn exercises. All may be played on a tenor with F attachment, but five are especially for bass. The last study on pedal tones is the only one with valve markings. These diversified studies require virtuoso ability to play.

REMINGTON, EMORY. *Warm-Up Exercises.* Pyramix. These exercises, which may be used as a warm-up or part of one's daily routine, help develop consistency of sound in all registers and improve flexibility. They include long tones, lip slurs, and scales throughout the harmonic series. Some of the exercises continue into the trigger range.

ROBERTS, GEORGE and PAUL TANNER. *Let's Play Bass Trombone.* Belwin, 1966. These 130 short exercises are for the young player who is past the beginning stages but unfamiliar with the F attachment. The book is well edited, although teachers may wish to vary articulations from exercise to exercise. The more advanced studies with large skips are good for the intermediate player. There are chart sections on the use of the E attachment.

STEFANISZIN, KARL. *20 Spezial Etüden für Bassposaune.* Pro Musica, 1953. Edited by Keith Brown, these are the original studies upon which the International Music Company edition is based.

STEPHANOVSKY, KARL. *Twenty Studies for Bass Trombone,* edited by Keith Brown. International Music Co., 1964. These are excellent studies in varied keys and articulations. Mostly in the middle and low register, there is extensive use of the valve and several low B_1's. Some of the exercises are awkward and quite difficult. This edition is based on Stefaniszin's *20 Special Etüden* published by Pro Musica.

STÖNEBERG, ALFRED. *Neue Umfassende Posaunenschule für den Orchestergebrauch.* Hans Gerig, 1954. Although in German and for tenor trombone, there are ten pages of Wagner excerpts for the "contra-trombone," and a position chart for "Die Contrabassposaune in F mit 2 Ventilen [with two valves]."

WILLIAMS, ERNEST. *Bass Trombone Method for F Attachment.* Charles Colin, 1958. Edited by D. Schaeffer. Secondary sources indicate this to be a good method for the beginning to intermediate student. It includes scales in all keys.

WILLIAMS, ERNEST. *The F Attachment on Trombone,* edited by Roger Smith. Charles Colin, 1956. These studies are from the Williams-Smith *Method for Trombone* and are intended for the young bass trombonist.

ORCHESTRAL EXCERPTS

Most of the following books include the third trombone part (bass trombone) in addition to the first and second trombones, and tuba parts.

BERNARD, P. *Orchesterstüdien.* Alphonse Leduc. (Bass trombone parts are in Vol. III and IV only.)

BROWN, KEITH. *Orchestral Excerpts from the Symphonic Repertoire.* International Music Co., (presently, nine volumes) Vol. I, 1964. These excerpts cover a cross section of the entire repertoire.

FERRARI. *Passi difficilie "a solo."* Ricordi, 1970. Several volumes dealing mostly with Italian opera.

MENKEN, JULIAN. *Anthology of Symphonic and Operatic Excerpts for Bass Trombone.* Vol. I and II, Carl Fischer, 1957. These two volumes include only the bass trombone part and are easier to read than other excerpt books. Vol. I includes composers whose names begin with *A* to *Si;* and Vol. II includes those from *Sm* to *W.* (mostly Tschaikovsky and Wagner).

STÖNEBERG, ALFRED. *Modern Orchesterstüdien für Posaune-und Bass-tuba.* Hans Gerig. These excerpts are a cross section of the literature with an emphasis on German literature.

STRAUSS, RICHARD. *Orchestral Studies.* Edited by Berthold. International Music Co. These excerpts are the Tone Poems of Richard Strauss.

WAGNER, RICHARD. *Orchestra Studies from Opera and Concert Works.* Edited by Hausmann. International Music Co. Besides opera excerpts of Richard Wagner, this edition also includes some Overtures.

SUPPLEMENTARY PRACTICE MATERIALS

BACH, J.S. *Unaccompanied Cello Suites,* edited by Hugo Becker. International Music Co. This edition is the original violoncello version and is not edited for trombone.

BLAZHEVICH, VLADISLAV. *Seventy Studies for Tuba.* Vol. I and II. Robert King Music Co. Excellent for valve work, these tuba studies remain in the extreme low register and are very taxing. The many B_1's would be good practice for transposing on a single "F" valve bass trombone.

DOTZAUER. *Exercises for Violoncello.* Vol. I and II, Carl Fischer. Mostly arpeggios and scale-wise material, the sixty-two *Exercises for Violoncello* are valuable for the development of technique.

DUBOIS, PIERRE MAX. *Douze Soli en Forme d'Etudes pour Tuba.* Alphonse Leduc, 1961. Written for the French tuba, these exercises encompass work in all registers.

GATES, EVERETT. *Odd Meter Etudes.* David Gornston Publishing Co., 1962. These twenty etudes are written in the treble clef and consist of odd meters with varied tonal centers (modal, twelve-tone, etc.). *Odd Meter Etudes* provide good preparation for clef study and contemporary literature.

GETCHELL, ROBERT W. *First Book of Practical Studies for Tuba, Second Book of Practical Studies for Tuba,* edited by Nilo W. Hovey. Belwin, 1954. Book One is very elementary but in the lower register and is valuable for developing an open sound and breath control. Book Two is a bit more technical and mostly in the trigger register. Students with breathing problems or new to the bass trombone will find these studies useful.

LANE, GEORGE B. *Concise Daily Routine for Trombone.* The Brass Press, 1970. These exercises, which may be incorporated into a warm-up or daily routine, help develop flexibility, control, and consistency in the upper register.

ROCHUT, JOANNES. *Melodies for Trombone.* Carl Fischer. For legato playing and development of a "singing approach" to the instrument, the Rochut studies are among the best material available. They should be practiced as written, then played down an octave for reading practice.

SCHUBERT, FRANZ. *Gesänge Album.* Vol. I (edition for alto or bass). Edition Peters. These are Schubert Leider for low voice (in treble clef) with piano accompaniment. They are wonderful for phrasing, legato control and experience in performing Nineteenth Century lyrical style.

TANNER, PAUL. *Practice With The Experts.* Leeds Music Corporation, 1960. Compiled and edited by Paul Tanner, these are diverse exercises submitted by twenty-five of the top studio jazz and symphonic players on the West Coast. The exercises represent the players' "pet peeves" and how to correct them. The George Roberts exercise is excellent for moving in and out of the trigger register.

TYRRELL, H.W. *Advanced Studies for Bb Bass (or Eb).* Boosey and Hawkes, 1948. This book consists of traditional technical etudes in the low register.

TYRRELL, H.W. *40 Advanced Studies for Trumpet* edited Nilo W. Hovey. Boosey and Hawkes, 1942. The same as the trombone *40 Progressive Studies for Trombone* (except in the treble clef), these studies are excellent for technique development and reading trumpet music (change to tenor clef and add two flats to the key signature).

WEISSENBORN, JULIUS. *Bassoon Studies* Op. 8, No. 1 and 2. Vol. I and II. Carl Fischer, 1941. These bassoon studies are fine for developing agility, general technique, and improving skips in and out of the trigger register.

SELECTED ARTICLES AND TEXTS
RELATED TO BASS TROMBONE PERFORMANCES

This list of articles is not intended to be complete, but represents a sample of outstanding contributions on various aspects of bass trombone playing.

BREVIG, PER ANDREAS. *Avant-Garde Techniques in Solo Trombone Music.* Juilliard School of Music Libary, 1971. Mr. Brevig discusses problems of notation, technique, and execution in new music for trombone. The music of Austin, Berio, Druckman, Hellerman, Lanza, and Ross is used as examples.

BRASS BULLETIN, INTERNATIONAL BRASS CHRONICLE. Jean-Pierre Mathez, editor. Scholarly articles and reviews of books, music, and records will be found in *Brass Bulletin.* It is published three times a year in French, English, and German.

BRASS PRESS, THE. *Catalog of Brass Recordings* (current edition). Presently the largest stock of brass albums available from a single source.

BRASS WORLD. Robert Weast, editor. Published twice yearly, *Brass World* contains articles, reviews; and lists of new publications, manuscripts, and records.

BROWN, LEON F. "Study Literature for the F attachment and Bass Trombone." *Instrumentalist.* XXIII, No. 11 (June, 1969), pp. 71-75. This article is a short discussion and annotated list of methods and studies.

BROWN, LEON F. *Handbook of Selected Literature for the Study of Trombone at the University-College Level.* North Texas State University, 1972. This is one of the most complete lists of trombone literature (in print and in manuscript) available.

CHRISTIE, JOHN. "Teaching the Bass Trombone." *Instrumentalist.* XV, No. 8 (March, 1961), pp. 39-40. John Christie's article is one of the best general discussions on the bass trombone. The topics range from choosing prospective trombone students to performance of the low B_1 on a single valve trombone.

CORLEY, ROBERT. *Brass Players' Guide to the Literature.* Robert King Music Co., 1972-1973. Mr. Corley, manager of Robert King Music Company, has prepared a valuable catalog of all brass music in print. Prices of published compositions listed in this bibliography may usually be found in *Brass Players' Guide to the Literature.*

FAULISE, PAUL and TONY STUDD. "Double Rotor Techniques." *Connchord,* XIV, No. 1 (October 1970), pp. 3-5. Messrs. Faulise and Studd, both practicing studio bass trombonists in New York City, have written a short but valuable discusssion on the possibilities of the double rotor bass trombone (tuning to F, E, E♭, D).

GALPIN, F.W. "The Sackbutt; Its Evolution and History." Proceedings of the Musical Association XXXIII (1906-07), pp. 1-25. A secondary source has indicated that this is an excellent article on the evolution and construction of the trombone.

GRAHAM, JAMES. "Developing Your Bass Trombonist." *Instrumentalist.* XXI. No. 11 (June 1967), pp. 49-52. This article on teaching techniques includes notated exercises as well as suggested study materials.

INTERNATIONAL TROMBONE ASSOCIATION NEWSLETTER. Larry Weed, editor. The International Trombone Association is dedicated to the artistic advancement of trombone teaching, performance and literature. Write for information concerning the newsletter and membership in the association.

KLEINHAMMER, EDWARD. *The Art of Trombone Playing.* Summy-Birchard Co., 1963. A discussion of all facets of trombone performance. Mr. Kleinhammer includes excellent information on disassembling and cleaning the rotary valve, bass trombone mouthpiece selection, and varied bass trombone exercises.

RAPH, ALAN. *Double Valve Bass Trombone . . . . and how to play it.* (pamphlet) King Instrument Co. Similar to the Faulise-Studd *Double Rotor Technique,* this pamphlet includes some concise and interesting possibilities for using the double valve.

WICK, DENIS. *Trombone Technique.* Oxford University Press, 1971. Denis Wick's text is possibly the best complete discussion on the trombone currently available under one cover. (See review in *Brass World.* Vol. 7, No. 2, 1972.)

RECORDINGS WITH BASS TROMBONE
Solo Performances

BOYD, FREDERICK. *National Trombone Workshop 1971.* Golden Crest Records Inc., CR 9006. This two record set of various trombone ensembles (with comments by the late Emory Remington) contains some excellent examples of bass trombone performance within a large group. Fred Boyd, a Remington student and member of the Syracuse Symphony, performs Walter Hartley's *Sonata Breve* for unaccompanied bass trombone.

KNAUB, DONALD. (no title). Golden Crest Records Inc., RE 7040. This solo recital consists of transcriptions and original works performed with piano and unaccompanied. It includes Samuel Adler's *Canto II* and Alex Wilder's *Sonata.* Donald Knaub is Associate Professor of Trombone at the Eastman School of Music and a member of the Eastman Brass Quintet.

RAPH, ALAN. *Trombone Solos.* Coronet Records. Alan Raph, a freelancer in New York City, is heard performing arrangements and original trombone music with piano (Vivaldi, Bach, Bigot, Rochut, etc.), as well as his own unaccompanied *Caprice* for bass trombone.

RAPH, ALAN. *Bass Trombone Solos.* Coronet Records, 1716. Mr. Raph performs original bass trombone pieces by Bartles (*Elegy*), Croley (*Variozioni Piccola*) and his own unaccompanied *Rock.*

ROBERTS, GEORGE. *Let George Do It.* Regal Records, ST 1073. This album includes four compositions for bass trombone and stage band by Larry McVey. This performance is by the Fort Vancouver High School Stage Band.

ROBERTS, GEORGE. *Practice Makes Perfect.* Dick Noel Enterprises. This recording includes Nelson Riddle's *Five Pieces for Bass Trombone* accompanied by the Academy Brass. A recording of the accompaniment alone is also provided for practice.

SMITH, ANDRÉ. *Electronic Music III.* Turnabout, TV 34177. André Smith, who performs Jacob Druckman's *Animus I* for trombone and tape on bass trombone, has performed with Stokowski's American Symphony Orchestra and the Metropolitan Opera.

STREETER, THOMAS. *Music for Bass Trombone.* Kendor Music, KE 9972. This recording includes orginal works by Christopher Dedrick (*Inspiration, Petite Suite, Lyric Etude, Sonata,* and *Prelude and March*), Manny Albam's *Escapade* (with woodwind quintet), and Richard Fote's arrangement of Bach's *Sinfonia.* Difficulty of works: elementary to virtuoso.

Trombone Ensembles

Emory Remington. Mark Records, MES 50500. This album was dedicated to Emory Remington by his Eastman Trombone Choir. Recorded shortly before his death, this is a fine example of "Remington Singing Approach" to both tenor and bass trombone styles.

Symphonic Trombone Excerpts, Vol. 1. Excerpt Recording Company, 3000 Trb. Famous trombone excerpts are performed by Glen Dodson, M. Dee Stewart, and bass trombonist Robert Harper - all members of the Philadelphia Orchestra trombone section. A score is included.

The Chicago Symphony Trombone and Tuba Sections. Educational Brass Recordings, ERB 1000. Orchestral excerpts, transcriptions, and original works for trombone ensemble (with tuba) are featured on this recording. Performers are: Jay Friedman, James Gilbertsen, Frank Crisafulli, bass trombonist Edward Kleinhammer, and tubist Arnold Jacobs.

ADDRESSES OF COMPOSERS
PUBLISHERS, AND RECORD COMPANIES

Allison, Howard K. - P.O. Box 224, Buda, Ill. 61314

Ammann, Benno - Faubourg St. Alban 43, 4000 Basel, Switzerland

Andrix, George - 12226 81st Street, Edmonton, Alberta, Canada

AR Publishing Co. - Room 301, 756 Seventh Avenue, New York, NY 10019

Associated Music Publishers - 609 Fifth Avenue, New York, NY 10017

Autograph Editions - c/o Atlantic Music Supply, Box 18, New Windsor, NY 12550

Bärenreiter Verlag- Heinrich Schütz Allee 29, 3500 Kassel-Wilhemshohe, West Germany

Bassett, Leslie - School of Music, University of Michigan, Ann Arbor, Mich. 48100

Belwin - Mills Pub. Corp. - Melville, NY 11746

BMI Canada Limited - 4 Valleybrook D, Canada Limited, Don Mills, Ontario, Canada

Boosey & Hawkes - Oceanside, NY 11572

Boston Public Library -Copley Square, Boston, Mass. 02117

Brass Bulletin-Box 12, CH-1510 Moudon, Switzerland

The Brass Press - 159 Eighth Avenue, North, Nashville, TN 37203

The Brass World-Box 198, Drake University, Des Moines, Iowa 50311

Breitkopf and Härtel - see Associated Music Publishers.

Brooks, William - School of Music, University of Illinois, Urbana, Ill. 62805

Alexander Broude, Inc. - 1619 Broadway, New York, NY 10019

Brown Collection - Boston Public Library, Copley Square, Boston, Mass. 02117

Brown, Newel Kay - 805 Laguna Drive, Denton, Texas 76201

Burton, James - 28 Greene Street, New York, NY 10013

Cameo Music - 1527½ Vine Street, Hollywood, Calif. 90028

Canadian Music Centre - 33 Edward Street, Toronto, Ontario, Canada

Carrier, Loran - Ballantine, Mont. 59006

CMP Library - (University Microfilms), Ann Arbor, Mich. 48100

Charles Colin - 315 W. 53rd Street, New York, NY 10019

Composer's Autograph Publications - Box 7103, Cleveland, Ohio 44128

Composers Facsimile Ed. - 170 West 74th Street, New York, NY 10023

Connchord - 616 Enterprise Drive, Oak Brook, Ill. 60521

Cope, David - 3705 Strandhill Road, Shaker Heights, Ohio 44122

Corner, Phillip - 145 W. 96th Street, New York, NY 10025

Coronet Records - 4971 North High Street, Columbus, Ohio 43214

Creative World of Stan Kenton - 1012 S. Robertson Blvd, Los Angeles, Calif. 90035

Date Music - P. O. Box 3166, Hollywood, Calif. 90028

David Gorston Pub. - see Sam Fox

Dick Noel - See DNE

Dillon, Robert - Music Department Central State University, Edmond, Okla. 73034

DNE (Dick Noel Enterprises) - P. O. Box 3166, Hollywood, Calif. 90028

Doblinger - see G. Schirmer

Downbeat Music Workshop - 222 W. Adams Street, Chicago, Ill. 60606

Dunn, Russell - 179 Stanton Street, New York, NY 10002

Editions Max Eschig - 48 Rue de Rome, Paris, France

Edition Musicales Transatlantique - see Theodore Presser

Editions Musicus - 333 W. 52nd Street, New York, NY 10019

Educational Brass Recordings - 1044 Forest, Wilmette, Ill. 60091

Elkan, Henri - see Henri Elkan Music

Enrico Publications - 3850 Poplar Avenue, Memphis, Tenn. 38111

Ensemble Publications - Box 98, Buffalo, NY 14222

Eschig, Max - see Editions Max Eschig

Everett, Thomas - c/o Harvard University Band, 9 Prescott Street, Cambridge, Mass. 02138

Excerpt Recording Co. - P. O. Box 231, Kingsbridge Station, Bronx, NY 10436

Sam Fox Publishing Co. - 1540 Broadway, NY 10036

Ferma Music Publications - Box 395, Naperville, Ill. 60540

Fischer, Carl - 62 Cooper Square, New York, NY 10013

Fulkerson, James - 46 Grand Street #2, New York, NY 10013

Gay, Harry - see Enrico Publications

Golden Crest Records - 220 Broadway, Huntington Station, NY 11746

Goldstaub, Paul - 125 Gibbs Street, Apt. #9, Rochester, NY 14605

Goodwin, Gordon - c/o Dept. of Music, University of Texas, Austin, Texas 78712

Grzesik, Christopher E. - University of Connecticut Music Dept., U-12 Storrs, Conn. 06268

Hans Gerig - see MCA

Haskett, William - 2000 Lenaman, Waco, Texas 76710

Hellerman, William - 90 Morningside Drive, #4J, New York, NY 10027

Henri Elkan Music -1316 Walnut Street, Philadelphia, Pa. 19107

Hofmeister, Friedrich - see Associated Music Publishers

Holdridge, Lee - see Seventh Century

The *Instrumentalist* Magazine - 1418 Lake Street, Evanston, Ill. 60204

Interlocken Press - see Ferma

International Music Co. - 511 Fifth Avenue, New York, NY 10017

International Trombone Association
   Thomas G. Everett, President
   Thomas Streeter, Treasurer, 1812 Truman Drive, Norman, Ill. 61761
   Larry Weed, Newsletter Editor, Music Department, University of Southern Mississippi,
      Hattiesburg, Miss. 39401

J.M.G. Publishing Co. - see Larry McVey

Juilliard School of Music Library. (Lila Acheson Wallace Library) - Lincoln Center Plaza, Broadway
   at 65th Street, New York, NY

Kam, Dennis - 2153 Aupuni Street, Honolulu, Hawaii 96817

Kelly, James - c/o University Band, U.C.L.A., Los Angeles, Calif. 90024

Kendor Music - Delevan, NY 14042

Kessinger, James - address unknown

King Instrument Co. - 33999 Curtis Blvd., East Lake, Ohio 44090

King, Robert - see Robert King Music Co.

Kliment Musikverlag, Johann - Leipzig, Germany

Leduc, Alphonse - 175 Rue St. Honore, Paris, France

Leeds Music Corp. - see MCA

Lemoine - see Theodore Presser

Malcolm Music - see Shawnee Press

Marks Records - 6010 Goodrich Road, Clarence Center, NY 14032

MCA Music Corp - 435 Hudson Street, New York, NY 10014

McAllister, Robert - 3725 W. Caron Street, Phoenix, Ariz. 85021

McCauley, William - see Canadian Music Centre

McVey, Larry - (J.M.G. Publishing Co.) c/o Chairman, Creative Arts Division, Mt. Hood Community College, 2600 S.E. Stock Street, Gresham, Oregon 97030

Molenaar - see Henri Elkan

Monoco, Alfredo Del - 622 W. 114th Street, #22, New York, NY 10025

Music Production - Box 381, Orem, Utah 84057

Musica Rara - London W. I. England

Nisula, Eric - Cherry Brook Road, North Canton, Conn. 06059

North Texas State University-Denton, Texas 76203

F.E. Olds and Son - c/o Chicago Musical Instrument Co., 7373 N. Cicero Avenue, Chicago, Ill. 60646

Oxford University Press - 200 Madison Avenue, New York, NY 10016

C.F. Peters - 373 Park Avenue, S., New York, NY 10016

Philippo - see Theodore Presser

Phillips, Harvey G. - MA 315, Indiana University, Bloomington, Ind. 47401

Pierce, Allan - 6539 North Portsmouth, Portland, Oregon 97203

Polifrone, Jon - c/o Music Dept. Indiana State University, Terre Haute, Ind. 47809

Pro Musica Verlag - Leipzig, Germany

Pyramix Publications - 358 Aldrich Road, Fairport, NY 14450

Regal Records - 7816 N. Interstate, Portland, Oregon 97203 (if difficulty, see McVey).

Robbins Music - (c/o Big 3 Music Corp.), 1350 Avenue of Americas, New York, NY 10019

Robert King Music Co. - 112A Main Street, North Easton, Mass. 02356

Rochester Music Pub. - 358 Aldrich Road, Fairport, NY 14450

Ross, Walter - c/o Music Dept. University of Virginia, Charlottesville, VA 22901

Rumson Music - see DNE

Schramm, Robert - c/o U.S. Air Force Band, Bowling Air Force Base, Washington, D.C. 20332

G. Schirmer - 609 Fifth Avenue, New York, NY 10017

Schwartz, Elliot - c/o Music Dept. Bowdoin College, Brunswick, Maine 04011

Seesaw Music Corp. - 177 East 87th Street, New York, NY 10028

Seventh Century - Room 301, 756 Seventh Avenue, New York, NY 10010

Shawnee Press - Delaware Water Gap, Penna. 18327

Somers, Paul - 44 Fairmount Avenue, Chatham, NJ 07928

Southern Music Co. - 1740 Broadway, New York, NY 10019

Summy-Birchard Pub. Co. - 1834 Ridge Avenue, Evanston, Ill. 60204

Swedish Information Center - Stim, Tegnerlunder 3, 111 85 Stockholm, Sweden - (Box 1539)

Swing Lane Pub. - Beverley, NJ

Tenuto Press - see Theodore Presser

Theodore Presser Co. - Presser Place, Bryn Mawr, Pa. 19010

Trump, James - 130 Foxdale Lane, Port Jefferson, NY 11777

University Music Press - Ann Arbor, Mich. 48100

Verlag Doblinger - see G. Schirmer

Western International Music - 2859 Holt Avenue, Los Angeles, Calif. 90034

Williams, Marion - Box 111, Pennington Gap, VA 24277